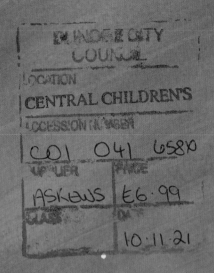

For friends, near and far,
you know who you are ~ RA

For Han x ~ FI

LITTLE TIGER PRESS LTD,
an imprint of the Little Tiger Group
1 Coda Studios, 189 Munster Road, London SW6 6AW
www.littletiger.co.uk

First published in Great Britain 2020

Text by Rosie Adams
Text copyright © Little Tiger Press 2020
Illustrations copyright © Frances Ives 2020
Frances Ives has asserted her right to be identified as the illustrator
of this work under the Copyright, Designs and Patents Act, 1988

A CIP catalogue record for this book is available from the British Library

All rights reserved • ISBN 978-1-78881-837-7

Printed in China • LT/1800/0066/0520
2 4 6 8 10 9 7 5 3 1

This Little Tiger book
belongs to:

_____

_____

UNDER ~the~ STARS

Rosie Adams   Frances Ives

LITTLE TIGER
LONDON

We gaze at the sunrise together
and wonder at all that we see.
There's a whole world for us to discover.
Let's explore it! Come on, follow me...

The world is a family:
we are all one,
Growing together
under the sun.

High in the sun-dappled treetops,
the branches all rustle and sway.
Squirrels are scrambling and chasing.
It's good to have fun and to play!

The world is a family:
we are all one,
Playing together
under the sun.

At times when our lives are so busy,
we just need to stop for a while
And make time for stillness and silence,
relax and recover our smile.

The world is a family:
we are all one,
Resting together
under the sun.

The sky hums with wings gently beating.
Songs float sweet and clear on the air.
We're free, flying high and exploring,
with wonders to see everywhere.

The world is a family:
we are all one,
Exploring together
under the sun.

In the calm and the cool of the forest,
cubs search for ripe berries to eat.
They share out the treasures between them.
Their friendship makes life taste so sweet.

The world is a family:
we are all one,
Sharing together
under the sun.

Being part of a family is special.
It means that we're never alone.
We all have our place in the picture
and the best place of all is our home.

The world is a family:
we are all one,
Living together
under the sun.

The stars in the sky twinkle brightly.
The moon's shining high up above.
We're so lucky to be here together,
in this beautiful world that we love.

The world is a family:
we are all one,
United together
under stars, moon and sun.

Discover the world
with Little Tiger . . .

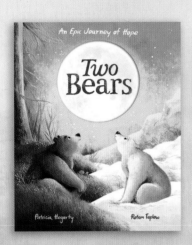

For information regarding any of the above titles or for
our catalogue, please contact us: Little Tiger Press Ltd,
1 Coda Studios, 189 Munster Road, London SW6 6AW
Tel: 020 7385 6333 • E-mail: contact@littletiger.co.uk
www.littletiger.co.uk